KT-553-038

CONTENTS

When the champions of Earth came together to battle a threat too big for a single hero, they realized the value of strength in numbers. Together they formed an unstoppable team, dedicated to defending the planet from the forces of evil. They are the . . .

JUSTICE LEAGUE ™

⟨ ROLL CALL ⟩

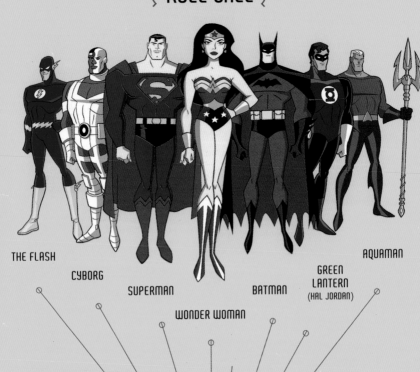

THE FLASH

CYBORG

SUPERMAN

WONDER WOMAN

BATMAN

GREEN LANTERN
(HAL JORDAN)

AQUAMAN

Newport Community Learning &
Libraries

X020774

AMAZO
AND THE
PLANETARY REBOOT

BY
BRANDON T. SNIDER

ILLUSTRATED BY
TIM LEVINS

raintree

a Capstone company — publishers for children

Published by Raintree, an imprint of Capstone Global Library Limited,
a company incorporated in England and Wales having its registered
office at 264 Banbury Road, Oxford, OX2 7DY – Registered company
number: 6695582

www.raintree.co.uk
myorders@raintree.co.uk

Copyright © 2017 DC Comics.
JUSTICE LEAGUE and all related characters and elements are
trademarks of and © DC Comics. (s17)

STAR39861

ISBN 978 1 4747 4903 9
21 20 19 18 17
10 9 8 7 6 5 4 3 2 1

A full catalogue record for this book is available from the British Library.

All rights reserved. No part of this publication may be reproduced in any
form or by any means (including photocopying or storing it in any medium
by electronic means and whether or not transiently or incidentally to
some other use of this publication) without the written permission of the
copyright owner.

Editor: Christopher Harbo
Designer: Bob Lentz

Printed and bound in China.

Newport Community Learning & Libraries	
X020774	
PETERS	09-Nov-2017
JF	£4.99

MARTIAN
MANHUNTER

HAWKGIRL

HAWKMAN

GREEN ARROW

BLACK CANARY

THE ATOM

GREEN LANTERN
(JOHN STEWART)

SUPERGIRL

RED TORNADO

POWER GIRL

SHAZAM

PLASTIC MAN

BOOSTER GOLD

BLUE BEETLE

ZATANNA

VIXEN

METAMORPHO

ETRIGAN
THE DEMON

FIRESTORM

HUNTRESS

CHAPTER 1

BREAK IN

"I'm *bored*." Karl sighed, resting his head in his hand. It had been a long morning.

Karl and his friend Sal were security guards at Benny's Storage, located on the edge of Metropolis. It looked like a typical warehouse, tucked away within a wooded area. Karl and Sal were happy to protect the facility, though they didn't know what was inside. No one ever came to pick up anything. They thought it was filled with a load of old junk that no one wanted. The outside of the building looked rundown, but the inside was a different story.

Benny's Storage was just a cover story. The facility was owned by Project Cadmus, a secret agency dealing in super-human threats. Inside were weapons and other dangerous materials recovered from the sneakiest villains on the planet. Neither Karl nor Sal had any idea what they were really guarding.

"What did you pack for lunch?" asked Sal, rummaging in his rucksack. "I've got a peanut butter and banana sandwich."

"Who cares about lunch?" asked Karl. "Don't you ever wonder what's stored inside this place?"

"Nah," Sal said, shaking his head. "I don't get paid to wonder."

Karl and Sal did get paid to make sure no one entered the dreary building. They had one other duty: never leave the checkpoint.

MEOOOWWW! An eerie feline cry came from the forest nearby.

"A stray cat!" exclaimed Karl. He rushed out of the checkpoint towards the darkened woods.

"What are you doing?" Sal asked. "You can't leave your post!"

"I'm sick of sitting here doing nothing. A cat needs help, and I'm going to save it," Karl said, disappearing into the bushes. Sal shook his head in disbelief. He couldn't believe Karl's carelessness.

RAOOOWL! HISS!

"Hey, Karl, you okay in there?" Sal called out. "I told you not to leave your post."

Karl bounded out of the woods, fearful and panicked. "Sal, RUN!" he shouted.

A long spotted tail slithered out of the bushes. It whipped around Karl's leg and swept him off his feet. He hit the ground with a thud. Cheetah emerged from the shadows of the forest, her tail wriggling behind her.

"Yes, Sal," growled Cheetah. "*RUN.*"

Sal stood motionless. He was too scared to move. "Freeze!" he said, fumbling for his Taser.

"Freezing isn't my thing," Cheetah said. Then she pointed to Killer Frost, sitting on a tree branch above. "It's *hers.*"

The chilled villainess leaped down from a tree. Frost could create freezing cold by stealing heat from the things around her. Ice was her weapon of choice.

"This place is a dump," complained Killer Frost. "Why are we breaking into it again?"

Karl took off running. He was frightened beyond belief. Cheetah wasn't about to let him get away so easily. She pounced on his shoulders, threw him to the ground and held her foot to his chest. He didn't dare move.

Killer Frost spotted two security cameras on the outside of the building. She blew them a kiss that fired off two sharp icicles, knocking the cameras out. "No photos, please," she said with an evil smile.

Sal grabbed his remote for the alarm from the checkpoint. But before he could press a button, Sal tripped and fell to the ground. Killer Frost cackled with glee. She blasted the device, trapping it in a block of ice.

"No!" Sal shouted. As he scrambled to escape, Killer Frost created one tiny snowball and threw it at the back of Sal's head. It knocked him out.

"Bull's-eye!" Frost cheered.

Cheetah hovered over Karl. He was shaking like a leaf.

"Don't hurt me, Catwoman!" he pleaded.

Cheetah growled. She didn't like being called the wrong name.

"Give me your finger!" Cheetah said, grabbing Karl by the hand. She dragged him towards the front door.

"I'm telling you, there's nothing in there! It's just a load of junk," Karl begged.

"One woman's rubbish is another woman's treasure," purred Cheetah. She placed Karl's pointer finger on the fingerprint scanner.

"ACCESS GRANTED," a computerized voice declared. The thick steel door lifted.

"Woo-hoo!" cheered Killer Frost.

"Once we get inside, watch out for traps," Cheetah warned. Her enhanced senses picked up something dangerous. She couldn't work out what it was.

"What are you going to do to me?" Karl asked. Cheetah head-butted Karl, and he collapsed unconscious to the ground.

Cheetah and Killer Frost stepped inside the facility. It was full of technology from across the universe. There were giant robots, massive ray guns and alien battle armour from the far reaches of space. None of it interested Cheetah. She was looking for something else.

"Whoa, look at all this stuff," said Killer Frost. She ran to a barrel labelled TOXIC SLUDGE and hugged it tight. "Just imagine what we can do with this! We could make an army of gooey little monsters."

A mechanical tentacle sprang from the floor below. Killer Frost yelped as it pulled her into the air. Cheetah jumped onto the wild limb and used her sharp claws to slice it to shreds. Frost fell to the ground, stunned.

"Traps," Cheetah reminded. She extended her hand, helping Killer Frost to her feet.

"What are we here for again?" asked Killer Frost. "I forget."

"When Lex Luthor went to prison, they took his old stuff. It's in here somewhere, and I want it," Cheetah explained. "Luthor made me promises and never delivered on them. I'm going to *take* what he owes me."

"Ooooooo. I love revenge," Frost squealed.

Cheetah scanned the room looking for Luthor's weapons, but she didn't see them. Instead, a big, red door caught her eye.

"There," Cheetah said. "That's the room we're looking for." The moment she'd been waiting for had arrived at last. The feline felon extended her claws and ran her hand across the door's slick surface.

"Yeowch!" the red door shrieked. "That tickles!"

Cheetah's eyes widened. She backed away as the door changed shape. It twisted and turned until it had become a human form with a familiar face.

"*Plastic Man,*" growled Cheetah.

"The one and only!" Plastic Man beamed. The flexible hero bowed dramatically. "I brought a friend too. Turn around and see!"

"Hello, Cheetah," said Wonder Woman. "I hope you'll both come peacefully. We need not resort to violence."

"UGH. I *hate* the Justice League," said Killer Frost. She clenched her fist to build an icy charge. She aimed her fingers at Plastic Man and bombarded him with sharp icicles. He swirled his bendy body through the air like a corkscrew, easily dodging the icicles.

Frost launched a second attack, but Plastic Man was prepared. He became a trampoline and bounced the dangerous icicles back at Killer Frost.

"Watch it, you rubber maniac!" she complained, batting away her icy creations.

"*RAOWL!*" Cheetah screamed. She swiped her claws in Wonder Woman's direction. The Amazonian princess dropped to avoid the attack. Wonder Woman swept her leg across the floor, knocking Cheetah off her feet.

"Stand down," Wonder Woman said to both villains. "I won't ask again."

Killer Frost ran towards the secret room. She failed to notice a taut red strand extending across her path. It was Plastic Man's leg. As Frost tripped, Plastic Man used his giant rubbery hand to snatch her before she hit the ground. He stretched his free hand into the secret room for something he could use to stop Frost for the moment.

"Got it!" Plastic Man said, revealing a freeze ray. He zapped the villainess, causing her to lose energy. She fell asleep in his palm.

"Sorry, lady. You get your ice powers from absorbing warmth. When I froze you, I took all that warmth away. I suppose you could say you're *out cold*," he joked.

Cheetah realized completing the mission was up to her. She leaped onto her hands, backflipping up and over Wonder Woman. Nothing was going to stop her.

But just as Cheetah landed, the amazing Amazon threw her Lasso of Truth and entangled the villainess. The pair began to tussle.

While they battled, Plastic Man wandered into the secret room. Inside were Lex Luthor's warsuits and other evil weapons. Plastic Man rummaged through the items, looking for something to play with. He came upon a spilled jar of grey material marked NANOTECH. As he bent down to pick it up, the substance came to life. It swirled through the air like a corkscrew, changing its shape in a variety of different ways. It mimicked Plastic Man's bendy abilities.

"Would you look at *that*," he said, poking at the little creature. "It's a little me. How cool! You need a name. I wonder what I'll call you."

"Plas!" Wonder Woman called out from the other room. She had defeated Cheetah and was ready to leave. "It's time to go."

"Coming!" Plastic Man said. He scooped the strange grey material into its jar and placed it back where it belonged.

"It's not easy for gals like us, Wonder Woman. Always scratching our way to the top," Cheetah growled. "We don't *have* to be enemies, you know."

Wonder Woman and Cheetah had been rivals for many years. Before an experiment had changed her into a villain, Cheetah had been a scientist. Wonder Woman wondered if the human part of Cheetah was still in there.

"There's a better way, Cheetah. You know that's true," Wonder Woman said. "We may be at odds with one another, but I believe there's good in you. Let me help . . ."

"*RADWL!*" Cheetah roared. "Leave me alone!"

A squad of Project Cadmus soldiers soon arrived to take Cheetah and Killer Frost to prison. Wonder Woman and Plastic Man boarded the Javelin, the League's spacecraft. They buckled themselves in for the journey back to headquarters. The Justice League's base of operations was the Watchtower, a satellite orbiting Earth.

"You really think Cheetah can change her spots?" asked Plastic Man. "She's *bad*. I say put her in prison and throw away the key."

"People can change. I've seen it. Growth isn't always easy but it's possible. It takes work. Cheetah could redeem herself and turn over a new leaf if she tried," Wonder Woman said. "*You* were once a crook, Plastic Man. Don't forget that."

Eel O'Brian was a small-time thief until a vat of chemicals turned his body into putty. Life was difficult for him at first. He then realized he could do some good in the world. He became Plastic Man and joined the Justice League soon after.

"Yes, I made some bad choices," said Plastic Man. "But then I realized my time was better spent helping people."

"If you can learn from your mistakes, there's hope for Cheetah and Killer Frost. Now buckle up," Wonder Woman said, taking control of the Javelin and blasting into the sky. "We've got to get back to the Watchtower for Cyborg's big announcement."

CHAPTER 2

WELCOME TO THE WATCHTOWER

"Hey, everyone!" Cyborg said, his voice echoing through the huge Watchtower satellite. Wonder Woman and Plastic Man parked the Javelin and made their way towards the command centre.

After many years of active use, the headquarters had seen better days. Its computer system had become sluggish. Thanks to Cyborg's tireless work, that was all about to change.

"Give me a second. I'm wrapping up some last-minute stuff," said Cyborg, his voice filling the entire facility. The man himself, however, was nowhere to be found.

Plastic Man twisted his head through the Watchtower's nooks and crannies, looking for his robotic pal. "Where are you, Cyborg?!" he asked. "This is creeping me out."

"Look up," Cyborg called out. He was hanging high above the command centre. A series of sleek, silver wires surrounded him like snakes. Cyborg waved politely and slowly lowered himself to the ground.

Vic Stone liked surrounding himself with technology ever since an accident destroyed half of his body. To save his life, he was given bionic enhancements. It turned him into half-man, half-machine. As Cyborg, he could talk with computer systems of any kind.

Part of Cyborg's role was overseeing the Watchtower's computer systems. He'd been planning something big for a while and was excited to share some news regarding the Watchtower's evolution.

"Nice work out there," said Cyborg. "You two took Cheetah and Killer Frost down with ease."

"I wish we didn't have to take them down at all," Wonder Woman said. "But crimes committed in desperation are still crimes."

"We're the Justice League. Taking down criminals is what we do," Superman said, returning with Green Lantern. They'd been handling a weather emergency elsewhere.

"I thought this was important. Where is everybody?" said Plastic Man, extending his neck up, down and around the League's roundtable.

"Let's see, shall we?" said Cyborg, turning on a monitor to show the rest of the team in action. "The Flash is dealing with an uprising in Gorilla City. A group of Leaguers are trying to stop a civil war on the planet Rann. Another lot of heroes are handling a crisis in the 5th Dimension. Bad things don't stop happening because the League has a meeting. Oh, and Batman said he's not to be disturbed."

"Sounds familiar," Wonder Woman said, glancing in Superman's direction. "Our Dark Knight does enjoy playing by his own rules, doesn't he?"

"He's got very good at it," said Superman. "We're ready when you are, Cyborg."

Cyborg flipped a series of switches on the command console and an array of bright blue holograms filled the room.

"Welcome to the new Justice League Watchtower." Cyborg grinned. The team moved around the room, studying the glowing images.

"What *is* all of this?" asked Plastic Man. He swung his head through the room, looking at each image with curious flair.

"This is *the future*," Cyborg said. "Our headquarters has seen a lot of action over the years. With so much use, our computer developed some bugs. I made it my mission to fix each and every one. Today, I've finally accomplished my goal. Not only that, but I've upgraded the entire system and added all kinds of fun new stuff."

"So *that's* what you've been up to!" Plastic Man said, wriggling his lanky body across the room, inspecting every hologram.

"I considered binning the whole system and starting from scratch, but that didn't make sense. What we had was amazing. It just needed a little love and affection," said Cyborg. "I fixed it and made it better."

Plastic Man shook his head in disbelief. "Why put in all that work? When something is broken just bin it and get a new one."

"C'mon, Plas. You know better than that," Cyborg said. "The Watchtower is state-of-the-art. No need to bin it when a simple upgrade can bring it up to speed."

Green Lantern's eyes widened as he moved through the holograms. "Wow. This is incredible," he said, squinting at one in particular. It was a very complex blueprint. "I may be an architect, but I've *never* seen plans like this. You outdid yourself, Cyborg."

"Those are all the brand-new features. Now we can detect certain kinds of threats before they appear. That way we can find out how to stop them," replied Cyborg. "Helpful stuff."

Superman studied another hologram with care. "The Watchtower now has double the amount of force fields, it seems. That looks like a good thing."

"You'll also notice I didn't add a single offensive weapon," Cyborg added. "Didn't need to."

"A battle simulator!" Wonder Woman exclaimed, pointing to a hologram. Noticing her own enthusiasm, she quieted herself. "I look forward to using that."

The team gazed intently at each of the mesmerizing holograms. They never expected such elaborate improvements.

WARNING! THREAT DETECTED!

A piercing siren sounded throughout the Watchtower.

"*We get it!* You detected a threat!" Plastic Man grumped, plugging his ears. "How about downgrading that noise?"

"The computer is sensing a dimensional breach off the coast of Florida, USA," Cyborg said. "ON SCREEN." A strange image appeared on the enormous monitor. A cosmic storm was developing. The skies were darkening.

"Jacksonville Beach is swirling with bizarre energies. It looks like a portal is about to open. Could be friend, could be foe, could be *anything*," Cyborg admitted.

"How come we don't know *exactly* what it is? I thought you said you improved this thing!" Plastic Man said, crossing his arms.

"Superman and I will head down to check it out," Green Lantern said, firing up his power ring.

Wonder Woman gazed at the stormy images. "Innocent lives are at stake," she said. "Protecting them *must* come first."

"Don't worry, Wonder Woman," Cyborg said with a smile. "Superman and Green Lantern have this one covered. We'll monitor the situation from here."

Superman and Green Lantern soon arrived on the scene to find electric energy crackling through the clouds. The portal opened wide as the winds picked up. A nearby van whipped into the air, heading straight for a family of holidaymakers. Green Lantern created a giant bubble to shield them from danger. The van bounced off the protective cover and into the ocean.

Superman spotted a little boy caught in a wind-whipped tide. It kept him from swimming back to shore, and he began to panic. The Man of Steel dived into the water, scooped him up and carried him back to the beach.

"Any ideas about this portal?" asked Superman.

"We're about to find out!" Green Lantern exclaimed. "Someone is coming through it."

A blazing light blinded Superman and Green Lantern. A sleek golden form hovered on the edge of the gateway. Its eyes glowed a deep red. With the flick of a wrist, the portal behind the commanding figure started to close. The winds died down. The weather patterns began returning to normal. The mystery man was revealed at last.

Amazo had returned.

CHAPTER 3

AMAZO RETURNS

Amazo scanned the area. His visual appearance made him seem calm, but looks could be deceiving. As an android, he couldn't feel human emotions. This made him difficult to interpret. His arrival had brought chaos upon the small town, but he remained unaffected.

Superman and Green Lantern knew Amazo was a dangerous foe. His body was made of nanotechnology. It allowed him to mimic the superpowers of any hero, or villain, he encountered.

Years ago, when Amazo was first created, his powers sparked the interest of Lex Luthor. The super-villain tricked Amazo into battling the Justice League for his own personal gain. The plan was a failure, but Amazo began adapting beyond his initial abilities. He was frustrated for having been used for evil purposes and considered a life of heroism.

After studying with Dr. Fate for a short time, Amazo took to the stars seeking knowledge. Now he'd returned to Earth with mysterious intent. Was he going to follow a heroic path or an evil one? Superman and Green Lantern couldn't quite tell, but the situation didn't look good.

"Tread carefully, Superman," warned Green Lantern. "There's an amusement park nearby. Lots of people could get caught in the crossfire."

"Good point," said the Man of Steel, considering Green Lantern's words. "Be ready to clear the area. In the meantime, we'll give our old friend a fair shake."

"Superman," said Amazo. His red eyes burned brighter.

"It's been a while, Amazo. What are you doing here?" Superman asked.

Green Lantern's ring glowed. He braced for battle. Amazo took notice.

"Do not fear me," the android boomed. "I want to help."

"The last time we saw Amazo he was on the fence about being a hero. It looks like he went in the opposite direction," Green Lantern whispered. "His voice sounds deeper, *angrier.* He's back to his old ways. We need to stop him before he does something."

"We *have* to give Amazo the benefit of the doubt," Superman said. "Reason with him."

The Man of Steel tried connecting to Amazo's softer side. "We thought that you'd changed for the better, Amazo," he said. "Your dramatic arrival has us worried."

"The end is near," Amazo warned.

"That answers our question," said Green Lantern, moving into a fighting stance.

"Wait," whispered Superman. "We need to find out what he wants."

Amazo's eyes blazed with power. "I can hear you, Superman. I can hear *everything*," he began. "I've travelled the multiverse in search of knowledge, experiencing things beyond human understanding. I've watched worlds live and die. My journey has brought me to a simple conclusion."

"That sounds promising," muttered Superman.

"Humanity must be wiped out," Amazo decreed. *"By me."*

"And there you have it," grumbled Green Lantern. "We've got a situation."

"You are afraid to fight me because I can absorb your powers and use them against you," Amazo said, taking slow steps towards his enemies.

Superman had stopped many villains, but Amazo was a special challenge. The Man of Steel couldn't reason with a cold, emotionless android. Amazo didn't care about human feelings or suffering. It left Superman feeling helpless. He didn't like it at all.

Amazo gazed at the nearby amusement park as if it were a shining prize.

"Oh no you don't," Green Lantern said. He used his power ring to create a thick cocoon of green energy around Amazo. The green prison lasted only seconds. Amazo sucked the energy into his body as if he were a sponge. A ring formed on the villain's finger, and he blasted Green Lantern with his own power. The Emerald Warrior went flying.

"You use violence to get what you want. I will do the same," Amazo said, zooming away like a bolt. He landed at the amusement park, hitting the ground with a loud **BOOM**.

Amazo ripped an empty Ferris wheel off its hinges and threw it at a sea of terrified tourists. Superman raced in to catch the gigantic ride. He grabbed it with ease and set it safely on the ground. Anger swelled within him as he turned his attention back to the task at hand: defeating Amazo.

"You're a failure, Superman. Earth is being destroyed by disease, war and famine," explained Amazo. "What have you done to stop it? Where is the mighty Justice League when people need them?"

"We're delivering medicine," Superman replied, gathering his strength. "We're helping people plant seeds that will grow into crops. We may not be able to solve every problem, but we do what we can to help. You've got a lot of nerve coming here and making threats."

Green Lantern saw Superman getting angrier. He stepped in to give his old friend some valuable advice.

"Don't let him get the best of you," Green Lantern advised. "You want to do something? Move Amazo away from people with a targeted strike."

"My pleasure," Superman said. He took off like a rocket, ramming Amazo in the chest. The massive force pushed Amazo away from the amusement park, hurtling him out to sea. His android mind raced as he tumbled through the air. Losing was not something he planned on.

Amazo soon stopped his tailspin and regained control. He noticed something curious. A naval ship was stationed off the coastline. He scanned it using Superman's X-ray vision. He spied a large stockpile of missiles and torpedoes.

"This ship contains weapons," Amazo said. "I will use them to conquer the planet."

"That naval ship is stationed here for protection!" Superman exclaimed, hurtling towards Amazo once again and knocking him far out to sea.

"You do not understand, Superman. You are an *alien*, after all," Amazo taunted. "Humans love destroying each other. Let me help them."

Superman had held back long enough. He charged Amazo, striking him with great force.

"Why are you doing this?" Superman asked. "I thought we'd moved past our differences."

"Alone in the far reaches of space, I felt an awakening," Amazo said, zapping Superman with a steady blast of heat vision. "I've *changed*."

"Not for the better I might add," the Man of Steel said, striking back with a blast of his own heat vision. It was a stand-off.

Superman and Amazo focused their heat vision at one another. It was an intense show of force.

As they moved closer, Amazo absorbed more of Superman's power. It left him bursting with strength. Finally, face-to-face with the Man of Steel, Amazo ended his laser assault. He grabbed Superman by the arm and threw him into space like a rag doll.

Green Lantern watched from nearby. He was afraid to step in. He now had no choice.

"Time to get serious," he growled, powering up his ring.

Amazo stole Green Lantern's power right out from under him. It energized him. A suit of glowing emerald armour formed around Amazo's sleek golden body.

"Yes, let's get *serious*," the villain mocked. He focused his power, creating a swarm of tiny green missiles. He launched them towards Green Lantern who used his ring to create a body shield. It protected him from harm.

"Now to use this ship for its intended purpose," Amazo said, diving underwater. He lifted the vessel from the sea and shook it. Green Lantern created an enormous pillow on the water below. It saved the crew as they fell from the deck. They were shaken but safe.

Superman returned from above. Using his super-speed, he raced through the ship to make sure there was no one left onboard. Once he knew the ship was clear, he lifted the big green cushion and moved it to shore. With the crew free from harm, he rejoined Green Lantern to face down their enemy.

"We've got to let rip on Amazo, give him all we've got!" pleaded Green Lantern.

"It's not that simple," argued Superman. "He'll just keep absorbing our powers. Amazo will keep getting stronger, and we'll keep getting weaker."

"Then what do we do?!" Green Lantern exclaimed. He activated his Justice League communicator to contact the Watchtower. "Cyborg! We need backup. *NOW!*"

Amazo heard the desperate plea. The evil android fired off a blast of heat vision that melted the communicator. Amazo held the naval ship above him as if it were a trophy. With his free hand, he blasted Superman and Green Lantern out to sea with emerald light.

RUMBLE!

Amazo believed he was on the verge of victory until an unexpected arrival appeared. An enormous sea creature rose from the sea.

SCREECH!

It let out a piercing shriek. On its back rode Aquaman, King of the Seven Seas. And he was *not* happy.

CHAPTER 4

CHAOS AND HOPE

"STAND DOWN, AMAZO!" Aquaman bellowed. "Don't make me tell you twice."

Aquaman raised his shining trident into the sky. The mammoth sea beast he stood upon moved its tentacles in all directions. The creature ached for battle.

"Hello, King of Atlantis. It's good to see you," Amazo said. "Kindly step aside. I'm ending the world." Amazo's grasp on the naval ship got tighter. He was preparing to use it.

"Why would I do that?" asked Aquaman. "The last time we met it was as allies."

"Stay out of my way," Amazo countered. "Earth is diseased."

"You will respect this planet, robot!" Aquaman demanded. The sea king used his telepathic power to summon pods of dolphins to surround Amazo in the water below. Together, they made a high-pitched whistling sound. It vibrated into the sky causing Amazo to lose his grip on the naval ship. He dropped it back into the ocean.

"I didn't want to do that, but you gave me no choice," Aquaman confessed.

Amazo hovered in the air. He soaked in Aquaman's power.

"I will control your seas, King," he snarled, taking control of the sea creature Aquaman stood upon.

Amazo used Aquaman's telepathic power to command it to revolt against its master. The massive creature jerked back and forth in anger. Aquaman lost his balance. As he fell, the enormous sea beast used its long tentacles to catch its former master. It dangled the hero in front of Amazo like a piece of food.

"Humans are worth protecting," Aquaman demanded. "Call off this attack immediately. If you destroy everything, you'll end up ruling a dead world. Is that what you want?"

Amazo stopped. After absorbing the fullness of Aquaman's telepathic abilities, hero and villain were connected for a moment. This allowed Amazo to see Aquaman's point of view in a new light. *Perhaps humans aren't the enemy*, he thought.

It seemed as if the tide of battle had turned. Then another member of the Justice League entered the fray.

WHOOSH!

Hawkgirl used the force of her mace to strike Amazo from behind.

"Sorry I'm late," she said. The android sputtered through the air like a broken toy. Hawkgirl plucked Aquaman away from the sea creature while their enemy was distracted.

"What have you done?!" Aquaman shouted. "I had Amazo right where I wanted him!"

"A *thank you* might be nice," replied Hawkgirl. "I just saved your scales!"

"Look again," Aquaman growled.

Amazo had healed from Hawkgirl's attack and absorbed her powers. A pair of enormous wings burst from his back. A shining mace appeared in his hand. He was ready to fight.

Amazo threw the mace towards Aquaman and Hawkgirl. Before it hit, a green shield appeared around the duo. It deflected the mace into the water below. Green Lantern had arrived.

"Thanks for the save, Lantern. What now?" asked Hawkgirl.

"We stay and fight," Aquaman answered.

"No, we head back to shore," barked Green Lantern. "There are people to protect."

WHOOSH! Superman barrelled through the heroes, pushing Amazo further out to sea.

"That's our strategy? Punch Amazo and run away?" exclaimed Hawkgirl.

"He can adapt to anything we throw at him," Green Lantern said. "What else are we supposed to do?"

Amazo roared past the arguing heroes. He headed towards shore once again. Superman followed closely behind. It was a game of cat and mouse.

"I guess we're going that way," Hawkgirl said, taking off.

Amazo made landfall. This time he'd had enough. He arrived in the Jacksonville Beach city centre and scanned the area. His stare was cold and angry. He began his rampage. He used his super-strength to overturn cars, tossing them into buildings without a care. He used heat vision to pierce the city's water tower, causing the area to flood. Frightened residents ran for cover. The Justice League had their work cut out for them.

"What a nightmare," muttered Hawkgirl.

"This is just a taste of my power," Amazo warned. "Now that I've absorbed all your abilities, I am unstoppable."

Using Green Lantern's power, Amazo created an enormous mallet. He pounded it into the ground with great force. The hammering caused a massive earthquake.

A nearby billboard shook violently and came loose from its anchor. The Man of Steel caught it with ease.

"Protecting the people comes first," Superman shouted.

The tremors created gaping holes that opened throughout the city. One crack in the ground threatened to swallow a little girl who was walking her dog. Hawkgirl scooped up the girl and took her to a safe place nearby.

As buildings crumbled, Aquaman used his trident to deflect rubble away from tourists. Each Justice Leaguer scrambled to save lives as Amazo continued his deadly assault.

* * *

At the Watchtower, Cyborg and Plastic Man watched the monitor with concern. They searched for a way to combat Amazo.

"AAAH!" said Plastic Man. "Are you sure you don't want to call Batman? Yes, he's scary, but that man knows *everything.*"

"I can handle this," Cyborg said. He'd used the Watchtower's new upgrades to run hundreds of mock battles looking for ways to defeat Amazo. He couldn't find a single one. "Amazo is pretty much unstoppable. We know that. But his new mindset makes him *unpredictable.* We don't know his next move."

"Watching Amazo change shape reminds me of this thing I saw when Wondy and I were at Project Cadmus," Plastic Man said, putting his hand on Cyborg's shoulder. "One minute it was a pile of weird grey sand. The next thing I knew it was bending all over the place, like me. It was so cute. It needs a name, though. What about Sandy?"

Cyborg's eyes widened.

"Plas, you're a genius!" he said, hugging Plastic Man. "That grey sand you saw was the nanotechnology that created Amazo. It must have got lost in the shuffle when Luthor's old stuff was put into storage. If I can get my hands on it, I can find a way out of this mess."

"Road trip!" Plastic Man yelled at the top of his lungs.

"Focus, Plas. Can I trust you to go to Project Cadmus by yourself, grab the nanotech and come right back?" asked Cyborg. "This is serious business. Everything depends on *you*."

"Of course you can trust me!" Plastic Man said, letting out a giant belly laugh. "I'm ready to go. Where's our ship parked again? Kidding!" Plastic Man stretched his long rubber legs out of the command centre and towards the Javelin's docking station.

Cyborg was happy to finally have a solid plan, but he needed more time. His teammates had been battling Amazo for a while and were growing tired. He had no other choice but to contact Batman. He knew the Dark Knight didn't want to be bothered, but the situation had become dire.

After a few taps on the keyboard, Batman appeared on the monitor. He was in the fight of his life against a group of criminals. The look on his face said it all – he wasn't very happy.

"Cyborg," Batman said, elbowing a crook in the face. "I'm dealing with an escape at Blackgate Prison. Is this about Amazo?"

"How did you know?" asked Cyborg.

"I'm Batman," grumbled the Dark Knight.

Plastic Man stretched his neck into the command centre, all the way from the Javelin. "See! I told you!" he cheered.

"Get going!" shouted Cyborg, pushing Plastic Man away.

"What do you want?" Batman growled, pushing one of Blackgate's inmates into a cell and slamming the door shut. "I'm busy."

"I've got a plan," Cyborg said, taking a deep breath. "Plastic Man is going to get the tools that I need, but it'll take some time to complete my vision. The League is already struggling. As soon as they make contact with Amazo, he gains their powers. They're hitting him with everything they've got, but I need time to work. What do we do?"

"Where's Wonder Woman?" asked Batman.

"She's here at the Watchtower," Cyborg said. "In case of emergency."

"Send her into the field. This *is* an emergency," said Batman. "Tell her to use some of that Amazonian battle training. It should keep Amazo on his toes while the rest of the team takes a breather. I have one other idea, but I'll handle it on my own. Batman out."

"I guess you're going in," Cyborg said, turning around to find Wonder Woman already prepared. She'd dressed in her Amazonian battle armour, complete with shield and lasso.

"I know what I must do," she said, gripping the hilt on her sword even tighter. "This is war."

Cyborg wished her well as she left to join her comrades. Time was running out.

CHAPTER 5

JUSTICE IS SERVED

CLANK! CLANG! CLANK! CLANG!

Wonder Woman's blade echoed as it struck Amazo's golden form. She'd been fiercely fighting him while the other Justice Leaguers helped the citizens on the beach.

When Wonder Woman hit high, Amazo went low. As a young woman on the island of Themyscira, Princess Diana learned many combat techniques from her Amazon sisters. She grew into an unstoppable force in battle.

Amazo presented a unique challenge. He was unlike anything she'd ever faced before. Slowing him down was difficult. She used every skill she had at her disposal, but it proved to be no use. With every strike Wonder Woman landed, Amazo evolved to outsmart her.

"I admire your battle skills, Wonder Woman," Amazo said, dodging the sword attack with ease. "You waste your talents protecting these mortals."

"These mortals are worth protecting," replied Wonder Woman. She threw down her sword. "How good are you at hand-to-hand combat?"

"I didn't think I was able to laugh, but your faith in your strength is humorous," Amazo said, cackling with glee. "You expect to defeat me with your hands?"

"I will defeat you with the weapons of the Gods!" Wonder Woman shouted. She flung her shield at Amazo with the speed of Hermes. He caught it with ease and, with a flick of his wrist, threw it back with force. The ancient shield hit Wonder Woman in the stomach and sent her flying through the air.

"I do believe I am beginning to enjoy this," Amazo said. Then a dark shadow moved across the sky. The android looked up to find a beast unlike any other.

ROAR!

A howl was heard for many kilometres. The mythical Chimera had arrived. It was a three-headed hybrid made up of a lion, goat and snake. The enormous monster beat its wings and lashed its tail with fury.

"Did the Amazon summon one of her pets?" Amazo wondered out loud.

The Chimera's serpent head unhinged its jaw and blasted Amazo with its blazing fire breath. The android was unfazed.

"Ah. I see who you *really* are," Amazo scoffed. "You're not a creature of myth at all."

The Chimera swooped in and grabbed Amazo with its sharp claws. The beast snarled in anger. Its snake-headed tail whipped around, firing venom in the android's face.

"Dramatic alien," Amazo said, using heat vision to scald the creature's paw. It roared in pain as it lost its grip. "You cannot fool me, *J'onn J'onzz*."

The ruse was over. The Chimera revealed its true form, morphing into the Martian Manhunter. Batman had contacted him.

"This must end!" Manhunter barked.

"Why have you not taken over this planet, J'onzz?" Amazo asked. "Your Martian powers are unmatched. I do not understand why you help these worthless humans."

"And you never will. The humans of Earth have shown me kindness and understanding. They are indeed flawed, as are all things, but I will not let you hurt them," Manhunter said. He stood his ground.

"You are not one of them, and you never will be," Amazo sneered. "You won't defeat me." He absorbed Martian Manhunter's powers and used them to disappear.

* * *

At the Watchtower, Cyborg had finished his work at last. It had taken him longer than expected, but he'd finally created an exact replica of Amazo.

The duplicate looked just like the evil android except for one thing. He was greyish in colour, mimicking Amazo's first appearance, instead of shiny gold like Amazo's current form.

Plastic Man helped Cyborg load the duplicate onto the Javelin, then the heroes made their way down to Earth. Cyborg briefed Plastic Man on the way.

"What's your plan, Cyborg?" Plastic Man asked.

"Once we arrive, it's your job to get our duplicate Amazo in front of the real thing," Cyborg explained.

"WHOA, WHOA, WHOA!" exclaimed Plastic Man. "Why do *I* have to go near that crazy android? *I'm very fragile.*" Plastic Man extended his arm and snapped it like a rubber band.

"Trust me, okay?" assured Cyborg. "All you need to do is make sure the dupe is close enough that Amazo can absorb him."

Plastic Man wasn't sure Cyborg's plan was going to work.

"What then?" Plastic Man asked. "Is our dupe going to rip Amazo to shreds with his super-strength? Or maybe he'll just tickle him till he can't stand it any longer?"

"You'll see." Cyborg smiled.

As the Javelin descended, Plastic Man watched out of the window. His Justice League colleagues continued to struggle to contain Amazo. The battle was frightening to behold.

"I don't know if I can do this," Plastic Man shuddered.

"You'll do great, Plas," Cyborg said. "Let's go and take Amazo down for good."

Wonder Woman, Superman, Green Lantern, Hawkgirl, Aquaman and Martian Manhunter were battling for the fate of the world. Their group assault on Amazo was having little effect.

"Give up," Amazo said. "It's for the best."

"Never!" roared Green Lantern.

"Humans tried and failed. They deserve to be destroyed," Amazo decreed.

"Who are *you* to decide that?" shouted Martian Manhunter.

Amazo's body filled with power.

"I. AM. EVERYTHING!" he bellowed.

SHAZACK!

Amazo blasted the group of heroes, knocking them away like flies.

Cyborg landed the Javelin in the middle of the chaos. He opened the hatch and extended the exit ramp. Plastic Man wrapped his rubber body around the Amazo duplicate and carried it outside. The Justice League was weary. They watched their trusted friend place the duplicate in front of their enemy. The moment filled them with fear. No one could predict how Amazo would react.

"Plastic Man, be careful," warned Superman.

"Don't you worry, Supes. I've got this!" Plastic Man said. His bendy body was shivering a tiny bit. He'd never been so nervous.

"Cyborg, are you sure this is a good idea?" asked Wonder Woman.

"I know it is," assured Cyborg. "Watch."

"Voilà!" Plastic Man said, presenting the grey duplicate to Amazo. "Snazzy, huh? He's not as shiny as you, though. And he needs a name. So, what do you think?"

Amazo's exact double stood before him. He didn't know what to make of it.

"What is *this*?" Amazo asked.

"Looks familiar, right?" Plastic Man said, coiling his body through the air. "He reminds me of an angry little android I know."

"You created this?" Amazo said. He pointed his finger in Cyborg's direction.

"Yes," replied Cyborg.

"Clever," Amazo said. He looked the replica up and down. "My very first form. How primitive. I've become so much more than this relic. Thank you for reminding me of my greater purpose."

Plastic Man glanced back at Cyborg. "Uh, help me out here," he whispered. "Turn this thing on or something."

"Wait for it," Cyborg muttered.

Amazo was done playing games. "You put up quite a fight, Justice League. I will give you that. But you failed to make your case. Humanity lacks the intelligence and adaptability to continue. They must be eliminated."

ZZZZZZ! CLANK! CLANK! ZZZZZZ!

The duplicate made a series of strange noises. To the naked eye it seemed to be breaking down, but Cyborg knew better. It was all part of his master plan.

"Your sad replica has failed," Amazo sneered. "Now I will absorb it and end this once and for all."

Amazo grabbed the duplicate by the shoulders and squeezed. The replica suddenly came alive. Its eyes glowed bright red.

"NOOOOO!!!" Amazo cried. His sleek android form shook as the power drained from his body. Plastic Man dashed behind Cyborg during the chaos.

"Meet my Trojan horse, Amazo," said Cyborg. "You love power, but this is just a big, dumb robot. The way *you* used to be before you became all high and mighty."

Plastic Man snaked his head around Cyborg's shoulder.

"So if the duplicate doesn't have any powers, what's Amazo absorbing?" he asked.

"*Nothing*," replied Cyborg. "Amazo is absorbing a void. It's cleaning out his system. All of the powers and abilities he's stolen are being wiped out."

The Justice League stared at the damaged android as he sputtered in shock.

"There's a special prison waiting for him at the Watchtower. We need to get him up there as soon as possible," Cyborg said. "Superman, will you do the honours?"

"My pleasure," said the Man of Steel. He moved at super-speed, punching Amazo at full force and sending him flying into space. "See you at the Watchtower." He took off into the sky after the wounded robot. The battle was over at last.

*   *   *

After a brief bit of well-deserved rest, the Justice League gathered in the command centre for a mission debrief.

"Here he is," Cyborg said, unveiling Amazo's unique prison.

A giant cylinder filled with liquid sat before him. Amazo floated in silence, his body connected to a series of wires.

"How safe is this thing?" Plastic Man asked. He stretched his body around the container and gave it a tap. "Can Amazo break out of here and hurt me?"

"Don't worry, Plas," Cyborg began. "His circuits are totally fried. Amazo's system was shocked into a trance-like state. He won't be causing us any more trouble. The cylinder that houses him is filled with a clear, thick liquid material. It prevents him from feeling *anything*, which means he can't absorb our powers. He's not waking up anytime soon."

"A human created you and a human took you down," Cyborg said, tapping on Amazo's tube-like fortress. "Didn't see that coming, did you? Guess you weren't all-powerful."

"Incredible work, Cyborg," said Superman. "It certainly helps to have a genius on the team."

Cyborg glanced at Plastic Man. "I can't take all the credit. I had help."

"What about this fella? He still needs a name," Plastic Man said, swirling his elastic body around the Amazo duplicate. "Since he did so well today, I think I'm going to call him A+!"

"Sorry, Plas," said Cyborg. "He's getting deactivated and heading to on-site storage. He has a few bugs that need working out. We can't take the risk."

"You know, just because something doesn't work correctly, doesn't mean it can't be fixed," Plastic Man said. He'd bent his face into an enormous grin.

"You're right," Cyborg agreed.

Plastic Man rubbed his chin and cocked his eye. "You know, I think those upgrades to the Watchtower were a good idea after all," he said, extending his arm around Cyborg and patting him on the head. "Nice work!"

"Thanks, Plas," said Cyborg. "I've got a few more improvements I want to show off . . . "

WARNING! THREAT DETECTED!

WARNING! THREAT DETECTED!

An alarm filled the Watchtower once again. The Justice League stood ready to face the next challenge, whatever it might be.

⟨ END ⟩

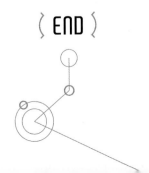

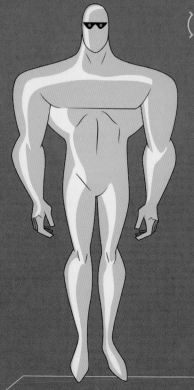

AMAZO

Amazo is an android that was built using experimental nanotechnology. His creator was a brilliant scientist called Professor Ivo. Nanotech gave Amazo the power to read a person's abilities and mimic them. After Ivo passed away, Lex Luthor adopted Amazo. He instructed the android to destroy his enemies. After Amazo absorbed the powers of the Justice League, he revolted against Luthor. He travelled into space to find peace. Sadly, it never came.

LEX LUTHOR   THE JOKER   CHEETAH   SINESTRO   CAPTAIN COLD

BLACK MANTA

AMAZO

GORILLA GRODD

STAR SAPPHIRE

BRAINIAC

DARKSEID

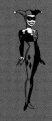

HARLEY QUINN

BIZARRO

THE SHADE

MONGUL

POISON IVY

MR. FREEZE

COPPERHEAD

ULTRA-
HUMANITE

CAPTAIN
BOOMERANG

BLACK ADAM

DEADSHOT

CIRCE

SOLOMON GRUNDY

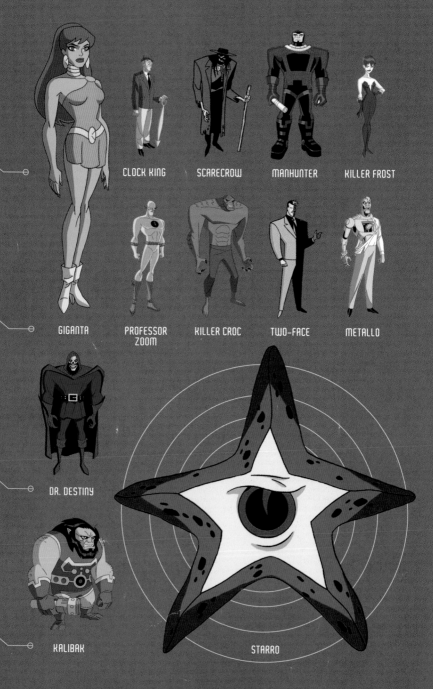

CLOCK KING

SCARECROW

MANHUNTER

KILLER FROST

GIGANTA

PROFESSOR
ZOOM

KILLER CROC

TWO-FACE

METALLO

DR. DESTINY

KALIBAK

STARRO

STRENGTH IN NUMBERS

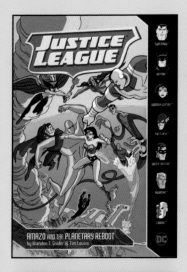

⟩ raintree ⟨

a Capstone company — publishers for children

GLOSSARY

android robot that looks, thinks and acts in a very similar way to a human being

blueprint diagram that shows how to construct a building or other project

hologram image made by laser beams that looks three-dimensional

interpret decide what something means

mimic imitate the look, actions or behaviours of another plant or animal

morph change in shape

nanotechnology technology that works on an extremely tiny scale

orbit travel around an object in space

primitive relating to an early stage of development

satellite spacecraft that circles Earth

simulator machine that allows you to experience what something is like, such as flying a plane or driving a car

telepathic able to communicate from one mind to another without speech or signs

THINK

1. Wonder Woman believes Cheetah can become a better person, despite her evil deeds. What are some ways we can all become better people?

2. Amazo thinks human beings are flawed. What are a few flaws that you have? Have you tried to change them? In what ways?

3. This book has ten illustrations. Which one is your favourite? Why?

WRITE

1. If you could absorb the powers of one member of the Justice League, who would it be? Write a story in which you use those powers to help others.

2. Create your own Amazo android! What powers would you give it? What would it look like? What would its mission be? Write a few paragraphs describing your Amazo and draw a picture of it.

3. Plastic Man likes to be funny, even when things are serious. Do you make jokes when you're nervous? Write about a time when humour helped you get through a difficult situation.

TH 14/11/17

AUTHOR

BRANDON T. SNIDER has authored more than 75 books featuring pop culture icons such as Captain Picard, Transformers and the Muppets. He's best known for the top-selling *DC Comics Ultimate Character Guide* and the award-winning *Dark Knight Manual*. Brandon lives in New York City, USA, and is a member of the Writers Guild of America.

ILLUSTRATOR

TIM LEVINS is best known for his work on the Eisner Award-winning DC Comics series *Batman: Gotham Adventures*. Tim has illustrated other DC titles, such as *Justice League Adventures*, *Batgirl*, *Metal Men* and *Scooby-Doo*, and has also done work for Marvel Comics and Archie Comics. Tim enjoys life in Ontario, Canada, with his wife, son, dog and two horses.